What do you have that God hasn't given you? And if everything you have is from God, why do you boast as though it were not a gift?

1 Corinthians 4:7, NLT

Fool Moon Rising

Text and illustrations copyright © 2009 by Kristi and T. Lively Fluharty

Published by Crossway
        1300 Crescent Street
        Wheaton, Illinois 60187

Cover illustration: T. Lively Fluharty
First printing 2009
Printed in U.S.A.

Hardcover ISBN: 978-1-4335-0682-6
PDF ISBN: 978-1-4335-0683-3
Mobipocket ISBN: 978-1-4335-0684-0
ePub ISBN: 978-1-4335-2282-6

Printed in Singapore.

Library of Congress Cataloging-in-Publication Data

Fluharty, Kristi
  Fool Moon Rising / Kristi and T. Lively Fluharty.
      p. cm.
Summary: The Moon learns the importance of humility and the dangers of pride after boasting about being the greatest light in the sky.
ISBN 978-1-4335-0682-6 (hc)
1. Stories in rhyme. 2. Moon--Fiction. 3. Pride and vanity--Fiction. 4. Christian life--Fiction.] I. Fluharty, T. Lively, ill. II. Title.

PZ8.3.F6824Fo 2009
[E]--dc2   2009000531

Crossway is a publishing ministry of Good News Publishers.

IMG		21	20	19	18	17	16	15	14	13	12
16	15	14	13	12	11	10	9	8	7	6	5	4	3	2

Astronomical thanks to

Lindsey, Lily, Madeline, Millie, and Tasya
Jon and Pam, Tony and Karalee, Rick and Delaine,
Kirk and Barbara, C.J., Gary, Stacey, and Lisa

Written and Illustrated by

Kristi & T. Lively Fluharty

 CROSSWAY

WHEATON, ILLINOIS

Dear God,

I heard a cosmic story
And wondered if it's true.
The Moon was stealing glory
And this is what he'd do.

He bragged each night that his great might
Could make the darkness flee.

And like a kite he scaled the heights
And said, "Hey look at me!"

The pompous moon would only croon
The songs that praised his name.
He hoped that soon the cosmic tunes
Would bring him greater fame.

It's really strange but he could change
His shape throughout the year.
His face would change, then rearrange
And sometimes . . .

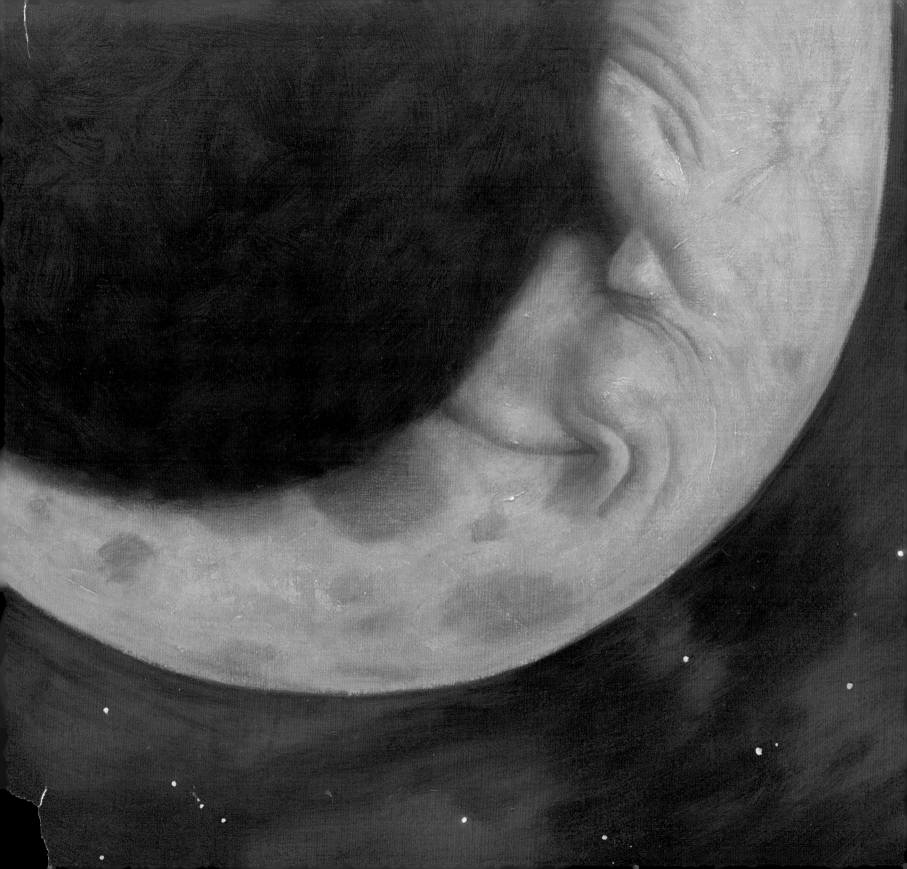

. . . disappear.

He loved the thought that astronauts
Had danced across his face.

And cosmonauts and monkeynauts
Would visit him in space.

He bragged that he could cause the sea
To rise and swell each day.

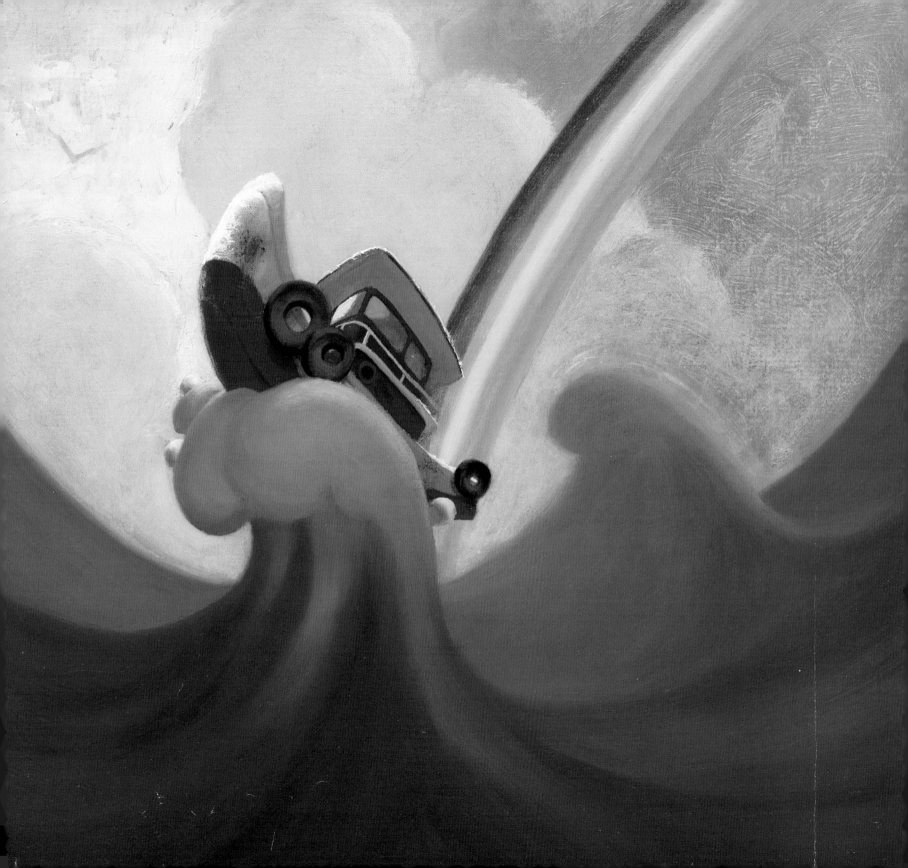

Then all could see how mightily
He'd pull the waves away.

He'd boast away and loved to say,
"I am the greatest light!"

Until one day a piercing ray
Showed him a shocking sight.

He saw his pride and then he cried
For all that he had done.
For he had lied when he denied
His light came from the Sun.

So now each night a new delight
Is what he loves the most.
Reflecting light with all his might,
The Sun is now his boast!

So God I pray for grace each day
To find the joy that's true,
In all my days and all my ways
In making much of YOU!

He made the stars also.
Genesis 1:16, NASB

The Whirlpool Galaxy

"X" Structure at Core of Whirlpool Galaxy

GALACTIC DIDACTICS

Why do you think the book has the title that it does?

What is the Moon doing that is wrong?

Does the Moon ever open his eyes in the story? When?

How does the Moon learn to stop being a fool?

What truth does the Moon finally acknowledge?